FORTUNE'S FRIEND

TALES OF RIVALRY AND RICHES

The Story Tellers by Winifred Moore

Other stories retold by:
Brenda Parkes: *The Royal Turnip*
Jane Pearson: *Fortune's Friend*
Janet Stott-Thornton: *The Magic Talisman*

Illustrated by:
Melissa Webb: *The Royal Turnip*
Mitch Vane: *The Magic Talisman*
Lorraine Ellis: *The Story Tellers*
Ester Kasepuu: *Fortune's Friend*
Designed by Peter Shaw

© 1995 Mimosa Publications

Published in the United Kingdom by
Kingscourt / McGraw-Hill
Shoppenhangers Road, Maidenhead, Berkshire SL6 2QL

Published in Australia and New Zealand by
MIMOSA/McGraw-Hill
8 Yarra Street,
Hawthorn, Victoria 3122, Australia

09 08 07
10 9 8 7

Printed in China through Bookbuilders

ISBN 978 0 7327 1564 9

CONTENTS

THE
ROYAL
TURNIP

Long ago, a poor soldier returned to the farm that he had shared with his brother since they were very young men. The soldier had been away for many years, defending his country against the enemy. Now, at last, he was coming home.

But his brother was not at all pleased to see him. "I have worked hard to make this farm prosperous while you have been away," he said, peering out cautiously. He did not want his poor brother to catch sight of the riches he had stored inside. "You go and make your own fortune." Then he shut the door in the soldier's face.

With the little money he had, the poor soldier bought a small, rocky field and a cottage that looked ready to tumble down around him. Day after day, he toiled alone to clear the rocks. Then he dug and hoed the ground. And, finally, he planted the field with turnip seeds.

The soldier watered the seeds each day, but the soil was poor and very few of the turnip seeds grew. But as these sent their young shoots up through the soil, the

soldier noticed that one plant was much stronger, and grew much faster than the others. It grew larger and larger. Soon it was bigger than the soldier himself, and still it continued to grow.

Never before had anyone seen a turnip plant of such magnificent size! When it finally stopped growing, four strong men were needed to pull it up and load it on to a cart. And two strong oxen were needed to pull the cart from the field.

"This is the king of all turnips," said the soldier to himself. "But whatever am I to do with it? No one will want to buy it, for not even the largest family could eat a turnip of this size. And anyway, it is too special to be sold just like any *ordinary* vegetable." Then he had an idea. "As this is indeed the king of turnips, I will give it to the king as a present," he thought.

The soldier drove the cart to the palace. People in the streets turned and stared as he passed.

"Oh, my!" they said.

"Have you ever seen anything like it?" they exclaimed.

"Why, that is a turnip fit for a king!" they gasped.

When the king saw the turnip, he was astounded. "Never in my life," he said, "have I seen such a splendid turnip! What is your secret? How did you grow it?"

"I have no secret," replied the soldier. "I cleared the ground. I dug and I hoed. I planted the seeds. And this is what grew," he said.

"If that is so, then fortune itself must favour you," said the king. "You must be a very lucky man."

"Indeed, fortune does *not* favour me," replied the soldier. And he told the king how his rich brother had shut the door when he came home from the war.

"When you fought for your country, you fought for me," said the king. "And now I shall reward you well." He called his servants and ordered that the turnip be taken down from the cart and replaced with gold and silver. The soldier could hardly believe his good fortune. He thanked the king again and again. Then he departed to begin a life of comfort and prosperity.

It was not long before the rich brother heard of the soldier's royal reward. He became so filled with envy and greed that he could not eat or sleep. As he tossed and turned in his bed at night, he wondered how he could add to his own wealth by pleasing the king.

"My brother gave the king his greatest possession – a mere turnip – and he was richly rewarded," he thought. "I can hardly imagine what the king would give me in return for gifts of *real* value."

Early the next morning, the rich man packed gold and jewels into his finest carriage. Then he set off for the palace. "Soon I will be the wealthiest man in the kingdom," he thought. "I am giving the king my entire fortune! What riches he will give me in return!"

The king was amazed at the rich man's splendid gift. "And now I must give *you* something splendid," he announced. "I will give you the most wonderful of all my possessions." Then he turned to his servants and said: "Bring forth the turnip."

The turnip was brought forth. The rich man's face turned pale. His knees began to tremble, and his stomach churned as

he watched the king's servants unload the carriage and carry away all his wealth. But all he could do was watch them go, and accept the king's "splendid" gift – and that, of course, was just what he deserved.

THE
MAGIC
TALISMAN

MANY YEARS AGO, a young girl named Rada lived with her mother in a desert wilderness. At last the time came when she was old enough to travel to the great city of Sambuka to seek her fortune.

Her mother, sad to see her go, gave her a parting gift of a magic talisman.

"I wish that I could give you a gift of safety and happiness. I do not have such a thing, but if you use this talisman wisely, it may help to keep you from harm," said Rada's mother. "It has the power to reveal footprints, even those that are old, or those that have been carefully concealed."

Rada put the talisman in her bundle of belongings, and set off for Sambuka. When she arrived, she found the city in great uproar. All the gold in the Treasury had been stolen during the night. People were huddled in groups on every street, busily talking and pointing.

Rada soon realized that nobody knew what had really happened. She heard all kinds of stories . . .

"It was a gang of forty thieves, all hooded in black, riding big black horses – I heard the hoof-beats!"

"It was a group of three men with the cunning of foxes, the strength of lions, and the speed of cheetahs!"

"It was the Great Red Shadow, riding invisible on the desert wind, who magically whisked the gold away!"

Most people took little notice of Rada, but as she passed the Treasury she found herself in the middle of a commotion.

"That's her. She's the one. I saw her!" Suddenly people were shouting all around her. She tried to break free of the crowd, but someone grabbed her firmly by the arm.

"I've got her. I've found the thief!" he shouted.

Rada was hauled before the Sultan. The plump ruler, clothed in jewelled silks, sat on a golden throne decorated with pearls and peacock feathers. But under all his outward finery, the Sultan had an evil heart. Not satisfied with the gold, jewels, palaces, and land that he already owned, he was still greedy for more wealth. It was the Sultan who had robbed the Treasury.

Now, to make sure that he would never be found out, he had sent his servants out to find a helpless stranger to blame for the robbery. No one, thought the Sultan, would care about a stranger.

For a moment Rada stood and stared in wonder, forgetting that she was accused of the terrible theft. Then the Sultan spoke. "You have robbed the Treasury of all its gold – gold which was to be used to build homes for the poor. For this terrible crime against this city and its fine people, you shall be thrown into prison."

Before she could utter a word of protest, Rada was dragged away and cast into a cold, dark cell. Alone and miserable, she could scarcely believe what had happened to her. How could anyone think that she had stolen the gold? She wasn't even strong enough to carry it – and just where did the Sultan think she had put it?

As the hours went by, Rada thought and thought. If only she could find the real thief. But that seemed impossible. If no one in the great city of Sambuka could discover the truth, how could a young girl from the desert? Then Rada remembered the magic talisman that her mother had given her. The real thief's footprints would be at the Treasury – and the talisman could reveal them!

Rada called to the jailer. She begged him to listen, and then told him that she could find the real thief, if only she could go to the Treasury – even if she had to be taken there in chains. The jailer was touched by the despair in the girl's face. He hesitated and then went away.

Finally he returned. "Only the Sultan can give permission for a prisoner to walk in the streets of Sambuka," he said. "Tomorrow at noon, you may stand before the Sultan and ask his permission. But be warned, if you anger him, he may make your punishment even worse." The thought of this terrified Rada, but she was determined to convince the Sultan of the truth.

The next day, just before noon, the jailer unlocked Rada's cell and she was led to stand before the Sultan for the second time. Once again he sat in his jewelled silks on his golden throne. He looked down and spoke in a voice full of impatience and scorn. "Why do you stand before me? What is your plea?" he said.

"Most eminent Sultan," began Rada, "I have been falsely accused of robbing the Treasury. I have no need for such riches, nowhere to hide them, and not even the strength to carry such an amount of gold. I can prove that I am not guilty of this crime if you will let me be taken to the Treasury."

"A ridiculous idea! I have never heard anything like it!" said the Sultan. "Take her back to the jail immediately."

But one of the Sultan's advisers interrupted: "Your Magnificence, perhaps we should give her one chance. It can do no harm to show your subjects that you are a fair man."

The Sultan was furious. He had thought that the theft from the Treasury would be forgotten, now that he had jailed the "thief". But it seemed that he would have to grant the foolish girl's request before the matter would rest.

"Very well," said the Sultan reluctantly. "You will be taken to the Treasury. You have one hour to bring the thief before me. If you do not, you will be returned to the jail and your sentence will be doubled."

Rada and the jailer lost no time in getting to the Treasury. The door was open and Rada held the talisman above the threshold. A crowd gathered around the door, and people gasped as several sets of shadowy footprints appeared on the stone floor. The footprints were all from the same pair of feet – the thief had come in and out many times.

With Rada leading the way, holding the talisman high, the people followed the footprints directly to the Sultan's palace. All were surprised to see the Sultan himself standing at the gate.

"Let us in. Let us in!" shouted the crowd. "The thief must be hiding inside." Rada looked at the footprints, and then at the Sultan, whose face had all at once grown pale.

"The r-r-rogue must have b-b-broken into m-m-my palace," stammered the Sultan. And with that, the people pushed through the gate. The footprints led on and on, through the innermost rooms of the palace, and on still further to the Sultan's most private courtyard. No one was ever permitted to enter here, except the ruler himself.

But Rada and the people behind her went on, following the footprints to the very edge of the central fountain. The crowd gasped. The fountain was almost overflowing with the stolen gold.

The Sultan quivered. The crowd was silent. Rada turned to the Sultan and held the talisman towards him. His footprints were clear all around him. The Sultan himself was indeed the thief.

"I have found the real thief," said Rada. And although the Sultan tried to escape, his footprints were clear behind him, and he was soon caught and thrown into jail.

The people of the city of Sambuka rewarded Rada with an urn full of gold coins. They even spoke of making her their new ruler, but Rada had already packed her small bundle of belongings, bought a donkey to carry her gold, and returned to her home in the desert. And there, so the story goes, she and her mother lived happily ever after.

THE STORY TELLERS

ONCE UPON A TIME, there lived three story tellers in three neighbouring villages. Their names were Rassim, Mustafa, and Hassan. Almost every afternoon, each story teller would sit in his village's market-place and tell a story. Crowds of people would gather to listen to stories of adventure, mystery, or romance. The tales were so fascinating that people came from near and far to hear them.

Each man knew about the other two, and all became curious to know who was the best story teller of the three. One day, Hassan invited Mustafa and Rassim to meet him.

"I have an idea for a competition," said Hassan thoughtfully. "Each one of us shall tell a story in his own village. There is nothing unusual about that, of course – but this time the stories shall be told in two parts: the first part, tomorrow; and the second part, two days later. We shall count how many people come to listen to each part. That way we will know which one of us is the best story teller."

"But why count the people twice?" said Mustafa.

"And why tell the stories in two parts?" asked Rassim.

"Well," said Hassan, "if the people listen to the first part of a story and find that it is not well told, they will not return for the second part. If the story *is* intriguing and well told, then people will return. And they will bring other people with them. We will know who is the best story teller, because he will increase his audience for the second part of the story."

"This plan will certainly tell us who is the best story teller," said Mustafa.

Rassim stayed quiet, but he agreed to take part in the competition. And the three story tellers parted to prepare their stories for the next day.

The next afternoon, Hassan, Mustafa, and Rassim settled themselves in the market-places of their villages and began their stories.

Hassan began a story about an Indian Princess who rode on a magic carpet to fantastic places.

Mustafa began a story about a sailor who set off to travel the world, seeking his fortune.

And Rassim began a story about a genie who had the power to grant great wealth to one person each one hundred years.

Mustafa and Hassan each drew a large crowd. The people listened intently, and as the first part of each of the stories ended, the crowds seemed eager to return two days later.

In the market-place in Rassim's village, the crowd listened with fascination as the story teller told of the great riches bestowed by the magical genie. Every listener imagined being the lucky person, and dreamed of how wonderful life would be with such wealth. As Rassim

came to the end of the first part of the story, everyone in the crowd was eager to hear the second part.

And Rassim told them that it would, indeed, be a special occasion. "In two days' time," he said, "it will be exactly one hundred years since the genie's last appearance. In two days, the genie will, once again, return to this very place to bestow great wealth on one person of

his choosing." The crowd left in a great outburst of chatter as they discussed who the lucky person would be.

Later that same afternoon, the three story tellers met as arranged to tell one another how many people had come to listen to each of their stories. When they compared numbers they were amazed to find that they had attracted audiences of almost exactly the same size.

"It seems that no one of us is a better story teller than the others," said Mustafa.

"Perhaps we shall find out that we are equally great," said Hassan.

But Rassim smiled. "The competition is not finished yet. We must each count the people who come to hear how our stories end," he said.

Two days later, the three story tellers returned to the market-places in their villages. Both Mustafa and Hassan found themselves completely alone; not a single person had returned to hear the second parts of their stories.

Everyone had gone to listen to Rassim. The market-place in his village was crowded with people, all eager to be the one to become rich.

When Rassim saw that not a space was left in the market-place, he began the second part of his story. Once more, he described the riches that the genie could magically bestow. While he spoke, a man of enormous stature appeared from behind a market-stall. He was bare-chested, and wore long silken trousers that billowed around his legs. He stood, arms folded,

carefully eyeing the crowd. The audience gasped and fell silent.

"Are you the genie who can grant enormous wealth to one person every one hundred years?" asked Rassim.

"I am," replied the swarthy figure.

"And have you chosen that person?" asked Rassim.

"I have," said the genie, pointing to a beautiful young girl sitting on a wall. The girl almost lost her balance in her excitement. "I will give you ten caskets of gold this very day," said the genie. "But you must promise to give me something in return."

"I would promise," said the young girl. "But I am poor; I have nothing of value to give you."

"You must give me your beauty," said the genie.

The crowd gasped. The young girl gasped. Then there was silence in the market-place as everyone waited to hear what the beautiful girl would say.

But she didn't say anything. She just jumped off the wall and ran, through the crowd and out of the market-place.

"I will choose another," boomed the genie. Rassim stayed silent. The genie pointed to a tall muscular man near the back of the crowd. "I will give you ten caskets of gold this very day," said the genie.

The man made his way to the front of the crowd and stood before the genie. "You may certainly have *my* beauty in return for the gold," he said eagerly.

"No," said the genie. "In return for such wealth, I want your strength."

"No!" protested the strong man. "Not even all the gold in the world is worth my strength. I would be too weak to enjoy it!" He turned and made his way back into the crowd. Rassim smiled a little more.

"Is there *anyone* here who will accept my gold?" asked the genie. The crowd murmured and shuffled uncomfortably. Only one person stepped forward.

"Would you choose me?" asked an old, frail woman. "I have neither beauty nor strength."

"I do not ask you for those," replied the genie. "I will give you ten caskets of gold in return for one day of your life."

The old woman considered the genie's offer for a moment. Then she said, "I am old and may not have long to live, but I cherish the time I have. How can I give you one day when that day may be my last? No, I will not accept your offer."

The genie gazed once again at the crowd, and then turned to Rassim. "You have attracted a fine and wise audience," he said to the story teller. Then he disappeared behind a market-stall as quickly as he had first appeared.

Slowly, the people in the crowd began returning to their homes. Mustafa and Hassan heard the story of the genie from people coming back to their villages, and hurried to see Rassim.

"Rassim, you have clearly won the competition," said Mustafa.

"Yes," said Hassan, "you are the greatest story teller among us."

Rassim looked at them and smiled. "Yes, I have won the competition. But perhaps we still do not know who is the best story teller."

"Why do you say that?" said Mustafa, looking confused.

"Well," said Rassim, "my story may have been well told, but that may not have been why so many people came today. Greed is very powerful and never fails to draw large crowds."

"But no one accepted the genie's offer of enormous wealth," said Hassan.

"No," Rassim smiled. "The people were wise enough to realize that many gifts we have are many times more valuable than all the gold in the world."

"That in itself is truly a remarkable story," said Hassan. "But was there really a genie?"

"And did he really have such power?" asked Mustafa.

Rassim smiled at his two friends. "That is for you to decide," he said. "After all, it was a story."

FORTUNE'S FRIEND

THERE WAS ONCE a man called Ivan, who lived in a cottage on the outskirts of his village. Each morning as he went to work in the fields, he passed a beautiful young woman carrying an urn to collect water from the village well.

Ivan admired the young woman for a long time. He asked people in the village about her, and found out that her name was Jana, and that she lived with her father in a house in the village. Ivan longed to know her better, and one day he at last found enough courage to speak to her. Instantly, they fell in love.

The very next day, Ivan dressed in his best clothes and went to see Jana's father. Humbly, he asked if he could marry Jana.

The old man was very happy. He liked Ivan, and he could see clearly that Jana was in love. But he also wanted to be sure that his daughter would not be poor. "I believe that you are a good man," he told Ivan. "And you may marry my daughter.

But, first, I require you to bring me one hundred pieces of silver. If you can do that, I will be sure that you can provide Jana with a comfortable life."

Ivan did not stop to think about how he could do this. He did not stop to think at all! "Yes!" he agreed at once. He was so in love with Jana that he was prepared to do anything to marry her. "What you ask shall be done!" he declared. But when Ivan got home, he began to worry about his agreement. "In all the world I have only fifty pieces of silver," he thought. "What can I do so that my small fortune may now be doubled?"

He thought long and hard all night. He could work longer in the fields each day, but it would take years to save another fifty pieces of silver. He could sell some of his possessions, but he had nothing of any great value. And his parents had died long ago, so he couldn't ask them to lend him any money.

Then, just as the first glow of morning light crept through the window, Ivan remembered his uncle – his only living relative. Long ago, Ivan's uncle and Ivan's father had been rivals for the love of one woman, Ivan's mother. When she chose Ivan's father, Ivan's uncle went away with bitterness and hatred in his heart. "Although I have never seen him, I will go to my uncle and ask him to lend me fifty pieces of silver," Ivan decided. And he set off as the sun was nudging its way up over the horizon.

After a day's hard walk, Ivan arrived at the village where his uncle lived. But when he found his uncle's house, Ivan was dismayed. He had hoped to find his uncle living in a large, well-kept house, with servants and many luxuries. But the house before him was ramshackle.

A donkey was tied to a post by the house. It was very thin and looked tired.

"You poor beast," said Ivan to the donkey. "My uncle is too poor to give you enough to eat." And he gave the donkey the last of the bread he had brought with him for his journey. The donkey brayed as if to thank his new friend for the gift.

When he heard the donkey, Ivan's uncle appeared in the doorway. He was very

old and stooped and he was dressed in
tattered clothes. "My good uncle," said
Ivan. "I am your nephew, Ivan. I came to
ask you to lend me fifty pieces of silver
so that I may marry. But I see that you
are very poor, so poor that even your
donkey is just skin and bone."

"Yes," said the old man gruffly. "You can see that I have no money to lend you. But you may take that old donkey away with you." He knocked the donkey hard on its bony rump with his walking-stick. "That beast is good for nothing and expects me to feed it. Take it and leave me alone." Before Ivan could reply, his uncle disappeared inside and slammed the rickety door.

"He is angry that I have discovered how poor he is," thought Ivan. "And yet I cannot go away and leave nothing behind." With that he took ten pieces of silver from his bag and left them all on the doorstep for his uncle to find.

Then Ivan untied the donkey and led it away. "First I will buy you a good meal," said Ivan to the donkey. "Then I will give you a name." Ivan stopped at the market in the village and bought a bag of oats. The donkey brayed gratefully and began to eat. Ivan sat down beside it. "I made this journey looking for a fortune," said Ivan. "But instead I have found you, so I will call you Fortune."

The donkey brayed loudly. And Ivan headed for home, with Fortune beside him. He felt deep sadness at the thought that he was still no closer to having one hundred pieces of silver to take to Jana's father. It seemed that she might never be his wife.

Weeks went by. Each morning, Ivan met Jana on her way to the well. How happy they would be, if only they could be married! And each day, Ivan made sure that Fortune was well-fed. Although Ivan was unhappy, the donkey was content.

Then, one day, news arrived that Ivan's uncle had died and that Ivan had inherited his uncle's property. Ivan was sad to hear the news. He packed a few belongings on to Fortune's back and set off, hoping that somewhere in his uncle's old house there might be something he could sell for the silver he needed. Fortune seemed very eager to be on her way.

But when Ivan arrived at the house he found it empty except for an old table and an even older bed. "My poor unfortunate uncle," thought Ivan. "He could not afford anything to make his life comfortable and pleasant." And he turned to go, leading Fortune behind him.

But the donkey refused to move. She brayed and brayed and stamped on the ground next to the door of the house. The more Ivan tried to pull her away, the more Fortune stood firm and brayed.

Finally Ivan sat down on the wooden doorstep. Fortune became even more excited and stamped at the step. Then it broke. A piece of wood flew up into the air, and beneath the step Ivan saw a large sack.

"Is that a sack of oats, Fortune? Have you been making all this fuss over a sack of oats? Very well, you may eat, but then we must return home." And Ivan began to untie the rope that held the sack closed. To his amazement, there were no oats inside – but pieces of silver! Fortune must have known all along that there were riches concealed under the step.

"Now I will be able to marry Jana," said Ivan excitedly. "My poor old uncle wasn't poor after all. But how sad it is that he hoarded his wealth and didn't enjoy it," he thought as he loaded the sack on to Fortune's back.

Ivan went directly to Jana's father's house and carefully counted out one hundred pieces of silver. Jana's father was delighted, and immediately gave his permission for Ivan and Jana to be married.

All the people in the village came to the wedding. They sang and danced late into the night, and Fortune brayed along with them. And Ivan, Jana, and Fortune lived happily and comfortably for the rest of their days.

TITLES IN THE SERIES